What's Right

Written and Illustrated
by Patty Presnell Kinkead

To Elliott

What's Right

Written and Illustrated by Patty Presnell Kinkead
Book design by Tara Sizemore
Published May 2014
Little Creek Books
Imprint of Jan-Carol Publishing, Inc.

Copyright © Patty Presnell Kinkead
ISBN: 978-1-939289-41-4
Library of Congress Control Number: 2014939784
You may contact the publisher:
Jan-Carol Publishing, Inc.
PO Box 701
Johnson City, TN 37605
Email: publisher@jancarolpublishing.com
jancarolpublishing.com

Jan-Carol
Publishing, Inc

"every story needs a book"

Acknowledgments

I thank God for all my many blessings and for allowing me to live in a country where I can express my opinions freely; my husband, Jason, for loving and supporting me; my son, Elliott, for inspiring me to try; and Jan-Carol Publishing for putting my ideas into tangible form.

Dear Reader,

I hope you find Stumpy's story entertaining. I enjoyed the opportunity to express my conservative views in such a fun manner. Although some things get lost in political dialogue, I believe the fundamental theory of working hard to reach our goals is truly the backbone of the American dream. I love the United States of America, and I sincerely pray for the greatest success of her future generations.

With patriotic pride,
Patty

Stumpy was a very good squirrel.

He worked hard, and he gathered more nuts
than any of the other squirrels.
Every day, Stumpy's mother said,
"Stumpy, you are a very good squirrel.
I am proud of how hard you work."

One day Stumpy had a terrible accident.
As he was running across the road, a mail truck ran
over his tail. Now Stumpy's fluffy, beautiful tail was
only half as long as it was supposed to be.
Stumpy was very sad.

The next day Stumpy's tail was very sore,
so he did not work to gather nuts.
Instead, when he got hungry, Stumpy asked
his brothers for some of their nuts.
His brothers happily shared their food with Stumpy.

After a few days, Stumpy's tail healed.
But Stumpy still didn't work
and still asked his brothers for nuts.
They were tired of sharing their food,
so they asked their mother to talk to Stumpy.

"Stumpy dear, why are you not gathering nuts?"
Mother Squirrel asked.
"Your tail has healed nicely."

"Oh, Mom," Stumpy said,
"I'm just not ready to go back to work."

"Well, Stumpy, I think you should go to the Animal Support Group meeting. You need to learn what's right," Mother Squirrel said.

The next day, Stumpy went to the group meeting.

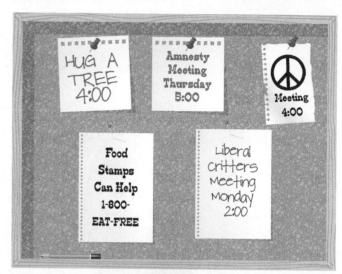

Many animals were there. To open the meeting,
Counselor Owl asked Gilda Goose to share her story.

Gilda Goose said, "I don't fly south anymore.
It is just too much work. Now I live at the park
and wait for people to throw bites of bread to me."

"Each year I have a new nest of goslings. The more babies I have, the more bread people throw to me."

"But lately, there haven't been many people at the park, and all my children are hungry."

"Poor you!" said Counselor Owl.

"Gee," Stumpy thought. "That's not right!
Gilda Goose should have planned better.
It's not right that her babies are hungry."

Counselor Owl then asked
Albert Gator to share his story.

"When I was a little
gator hatchling,
my daddy chased
me out of the
nest and tried to
hurt me. I was
very scared and
unhappy."

"Now that I'm a grown-up gator, Mrs. Gator and I have a big nest of babies each year. Every time the eggs hatch, I chase the babies and try to hurt them."

"I just can't help myself! It's all because of how my daddy treated me!" said Albert Gator.

"Poor you!" said Counselor Owl.

"Gee," thought Stumpy. "It's not right that Albert Gator tries to hurt his babies. He remembers how sad and scared he was when his daddy tried to hurt him."

Counselor Owl then asked
Bethany Beaver to share her story.

"It's not fair that I live in such a small dam when Baxter Beaver has such a large, roomy dam. I dropped out of Gnawing School when I was just a kit. It was too much work, so I never learned how to gnaw down big trees."

"Baxter graduated first in his class from Gnawing School, so he can chew down really big trees to build his dam. I'm just so angry that his home is better than mine. He shouldn't have such a nice dam!"

"Poor you!" said Counselor Owl.

"Gee," thought Stumpy. "That's not right!
It's not right that Bethany Beaver is angry
she doesn't have a larger dam. Baxter worked hard
to learn how to gnaw down really big trees.
He has earned his bigger dam."

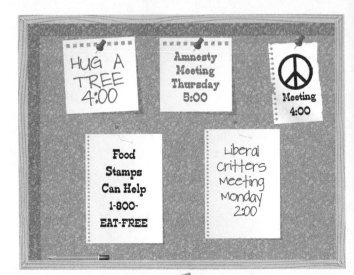

Counselor Owl then looked at Stumpy and said,
"It's your turn to tell your story."

But Stumpy had heard enough.
He knew what he had to do.
He had to go and gather nuts!

Stumpy raced home
and went straight to work.

That night, Mother Squirrel praised Stumpy.
She said, "Oh, Stumpy! You have worked
very hard today, and once again you have
gathered more nuts than any of the other squirrels."
I am so proud of you! Did your meeting help
you learn what's right and what's not right?"

"Yes," said Stumpy. "I learned it's not right
to take your brothers' food when you don't work."

"It's not right to have babies and not take care of them."

"It's not right to blame
your daddy when you're mean."

"It's not right to be angry because others stayed in school and earned better homes than you have."

"All of these things are just not right.
Working hard and taking responsibility
for yourself is what's right—"

"and I, Stumpy the squirrel,
want to be Right!"

CPSIA information can be obtained at www.ICGtesting.com
Printed in the USA
LVOW02s2257110614

389541LV00002B/2/P